Dash

By Elizabeth Mills

Illustrated by Jacqueline Rogers

SCHOLASTIC INC.

New York   Toronto   London   Auckland
Sydney   Mexico City   New Delhi   Hong Kong

A Marie Komajda–
au pas, au trot, et au galop, j'espère que tu auras
toujours de belles aventures à cheval!
—E. M.

For Gaby
—J. R.

Library of Congress Cataloging-in-Publication Data is available.

ISBN: 978-0-545-16584-6

Copyright © 2009 by Reeves International, Inc.
All rights reserved. Published by Scholastic Inc.
BREYER, STABLEMATES, and BREYER logos are trademarks and/or registered
trademarks of Reeves International, Inc.
SCHOLASTIC, CARTWHEEL BOOKS, and associated logos are trademarks and/or
registered trademarks of Scholastic Inc.

10 9 8 7 6 5 4 3 2   10 11 12 13 14/0
Printed in the U.S.A.   40
This edition first printing, March 2010

Table of Contents

Rodeo Day

"**G**o, Mike, go!" Jenny shouted.

Her brother slid his horse to a stop.

It was perfect!

The crowd cheered and Jenny clapped.

The rodeo was busy and loud. There were lots of people. Many wore chaps, hats, and boots.

Jenny and her dad walked to another arena. There was a girl racing her horse around big barrels. She leaned left and right, and rode very fast.

Jenny wanted to try this.

She went up to the girl. "Hi, I'm Jenny," she said. "You were amazing!"

"Thanks," the girl said. "I'm Hope. And this is Duke. Are you a barrel racer, too?"

"No, but I want to learn!" said Jenny. "I've been riding for five years and this looks like fun!"

"Well, barrel racing is lots of fun," said Hope. "But it is also hard. You have to go as fast as you can. You can't hit a barrel or go the wrong way. It takes a lot of practice."

"How did you learn to barrel race?" Jenny asked.

"I learned from my trainer, Sam," said Hope. "Maybe she could teach you."

Jenny's dad joined them. "Hello, Sam," he said. "It is good to see you again."

"Dad, can I learn barrel racing with Sam?" Jenny asked.

"Sure, Jenny," said her dad. "And I think I have just the horse for you to ride."

"We can start tomorrow at your ranch, Jenny," said Sam.

"Thank you!" said Jenny. "I can't wait!"

Meet Dash

The next day, Jenny and her dad went into the barn. The horses nickered and snorted in their stalls.

These were her father's champion Quarter Horses. They had names like Black Jack, Farmer, Goose, Nugget, and Indigo.

In one stall was a small Quarter Horse.

"His name is Dash," her dad said. "He's not working out as a reiner. I was planning to sell him, but he might make a good barrel racer."

"Hi there," she said softly. "Would you like to barrel race with me?" she asked.

Dash nickered and nuzzled Jenny's pockets looking for treats.

Jenny and her dad laughed.

Jenny got Dash ready and mounted him.
She slowly rode him out of the barn and into
the ring. His walk was very smooth.

She led him into a slow lope.

"So far, so good," she said.

Then Jenny asked Dash to gallop. "Wheee!" Jenny shouted. Dash loved to run! He would be perfect for barrel racing.

Practice, Practice

"They should be here any minute now," said Jenny's dad. "It's two o'clock."

A few minutes later, a trailer drove up. Sam and Hope got out.

"Hi, Jenny," Sam said. "Ready to start running barrels?"

"Yes!" Jenny said. "Dash is ready, too!"

"Here are the rules," said Sam. "The course is called a cloverleaf pattern. You have to ride the course as fast as you can. Don't hit any barrels or go the wrong way around them. If you do, the judges will add five seconds to your time. The clock starts when you enter the arena and it stops when you leave."

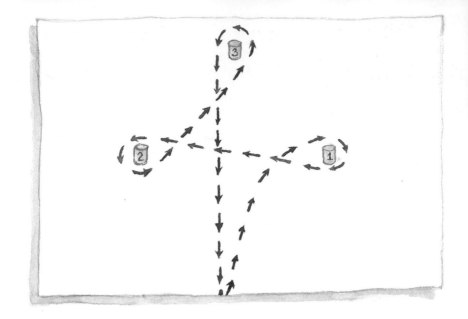

Sam set up three bales of hay.

"First, Hope will show you how to go around the hay bales," said Sam. "Follow this simple map."

Hope and Duke rode slowly around the left side of the first hay bale. Then they rode around the right side of the second hay bale. They rode around the right side of the third hay bale. Then they walked out of the ring.

"Now it's your turn," said Sam. "As you ride, lean into each hay bale to go faster. But remember, don't lean too far."

Jenny led Dash into the ring. They walked around the first hay bale, the second hay bale, the third hay bale, and out of the ring.

"Great job!" said Sam. "Let's try it a litt
faster now."

Jenny led Dash through the course at
a lope. But this time, Jenny went the wrong
way around the second hay bale.

Then Dash hit his knee on the third hay bale.

"I'm sorry, Dash," Jenny said.

"It's okay," Hope said. "I always used to forget which way to go."

"Keep practicing," said Sam. "You'll get better."

Jenny and Dash practiced every day.

Jenny's dad bought real barrels for them to use.

They walked the course. They loped through the course.

Jenny could tell Dash liked barrel racing. But it was so hard to remember which way to go. And when she forgot, Dash hit his shoulder on a barrel.

"This is harder than I thought!" Jenny said to Dash.

After a while, things got better.

Jenny and Dash learned the course. She
leaned Dash into the barrels. She kept her
legs close to the saddle.

She held on to the horn with one hand.
She used her other hand to guide Dash.

Jenny was getting excited for the race.

It was the day before the rodeo. And now Jenny was nervous.

"I feel ready," she said. "But what if I forget which way to go?"

"I was nervous before my first barrel race," said Hope.

"Just trust Dash and trust yourself," said Sam. "You two are a team. You'll be great together!"

Barrels of Fun!

The next morning, Jenny put on her fancy shirt, her new chaps, and her favorite cowgirl hat.

In the stall, Jenny put on Dash's halter. Then she showed Dash a colorful blanket. "This is from Hope," she told Dash. "It's for good luck!"

She brushed his coat, mane, and tail.

Finally, her dad helped her load him into the trailer, and off they went.

This rodeo was much bigger. There were so many people. Jenny smelled funnel cakes and fries. She heard loud music.

Her hands were sweaty and her stomach felt jumpy.

Jenny and Hope went to the barrel-racing arena. Two girls were ahead of Jenny. They did well, but both girls hit the last barrel. They shook their heads as they walked out of the arena.

"You'll do great!" said Hope. She gave Jenny a quick hug.

Now it was Jenny's turn. She mounted Dash and walked him to the entrance.

She took a deep breath.

"We can do it, Dash," she whispered in his ear. Then she led Dash into a gallop.

He was so fast! They raced around the first barrel. Dash came close but he didn't touch it.

Then they raced to the second barrel. This time, they went around perfectly. Jenny's stomach felt fine. She was having fun!

As they galloped to the third barrel,
Jenny took a deep breath. She held her
legs in.

Dash moved smoothly around the
barrel. And they circled it without hitting it.

Then they raced back through the middle of the arena to the exit. Dash's hooves moved faster and faster.

At last they were through the gate.

"You looked great!" said Hope.

"That was fun!" shouted Jenny.

Just then, they heard the announcement. "First place, Jenny Tucker and Dash!"

Jenny threw her hat in the air and shouted, "I won! I won! Thank you, Hope and Sam! Thanks, Dad! And thank you, Dash!"

BARREL-DIV-3 TIME
1 JENNY TUCKER 16:08
2 LISA WEST 16:97
3 GABY NEVIN 116:99
4 ROXY SUTTER 07:12
5 KORY WRIGHT 17:34
6 TAYLOR HILL 17:48

About the Horse

Facts about American Quarter Horses:

1. American Quarter Horses are called "quarter" horses because they can run a quarter of a mile faster than any other horse.

2. They are the world's most popular breed of horse. Today, nearly five million American Quarter Horses have been registered and they can be found in more than 80 countries.

3. The American Quarter Horse is the horse that is most commonly used for rodeo events like barrel racing, roping, and cutting.

4. The American Quarter Horse was the breed that helped to settle the American West. Cowboys used them to herd cattle, to pull wagons, and to ride around the ranch.

5. The American Quarter Horse Association is the breed registry for all American Quarter Horses worldwide. Each year, 150,000 new foal are registered.

Facts about Barrel Racing:

1. Barrel racing is a rodeo sport because it is most often held at rodeo events.

2. Barrel racing is a timed event, where the horse and rider ride around three barrels in a cloverleaf pattern. The fastest time without knocking the barrels over wins.

3. Although barrel racing is considered a women's sport, men and boys barrel race as well.

4. Rodeo events for children are often called PeeWee events.

5. The biggest barrel racing events for kids are held at the National Littl Britches Rodeo Finals and the National High School Rodeo Finals.

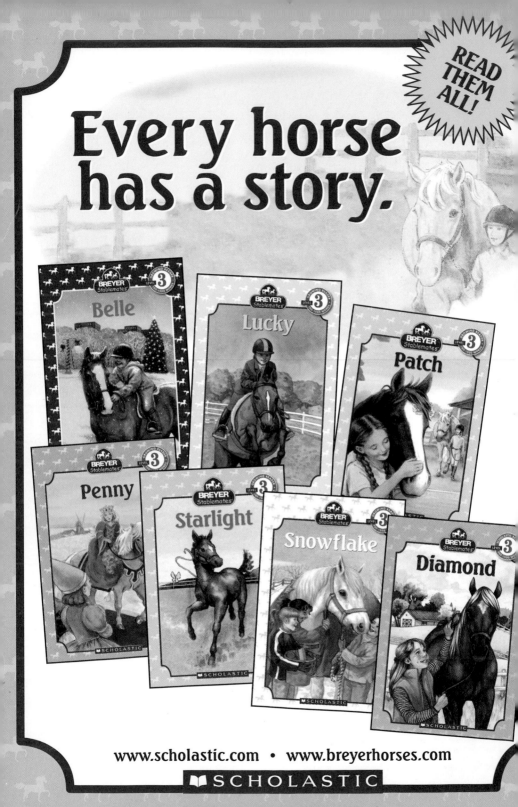